LOOK AND FIND®

Disney · PIXAR
RATATOUILLE
(rat·a·too·ee)

Illustrated by Art Mawhinney and the Disney Storybook Artists
Inspired by the art and character designs created by Pixar

Published by Louis Weber, C.E.O.
Publications International, Ltd.
7373 North Cicero Avenue, Lincolnwood, Illinois 60712
Ground Floor, 59 Gloucester Place, London W1U 8JJ

Customer Service: 1-800-595-8484
or customer_service@pilbooks.com

www.pilbooks.com

Manufactured in China.

8 7 6 5 4 3 2 1

ISBN-13: 978-1-4127-8003-2
ISBN-10: 1-4127-8003-9

Here we are in the French countryside. The sun is shining and the rats are hungry. Remy, the rat with the keenest nose, must sniff each bit of food to make sure it isn't poisoned. But Remy doesn't care for most of the food brought by the other rats. Look for these unsavory morsels.

Fish bones

Old grapes

Melon rind

Apple core

Potato peel

Drumstick

Candy bar

POISON

Remy discovers he is in the elegant city of Paris, near Gusteau's restaurant. High above the bustling streets, Remy looks down on all the metropolis has to offer. Look for these food-related shops that might excite Remy.

CAFÉ

CHOCOLATIER

BRASSERIE

CHARCUTERIE

PATISSERIE

TRAITEUR

La Boulangerie

Inspired by the busy kitchen at Gusteau's, Remy has decided to fix a savory soup. As his delicious pot simmers on the stove, look for these various kitchen utensils that gourmet chefs keep around a well-stocked kitchen.

Rolling pin

Mandolin

Salt cellar

Bread knife

Cheese knife

Mezzaluna

Hoping he can make the young man into a chef, Remy has come to Linguini's apartment for a quick course in culinary competence. While the capable rodent guides his blindfolded pupil, look around the apartment for some of Linguini's belongings.

Soda can

Bike

Running shoes

Soccer ball

Comic book

Cereal box

Tennis racket

Remy has returned! Reunited with his father, Django, and the rest of the rat colony, Remy finds himself in the middle of a celebration. Look around the sewer party for these rat-band members and their musical instruments.

Drinking-straw flute

Paper-clip harp

Nut-shell Violin

Salt-shaker maraca

Homemade horn

Rubber-band bass fiddle

Sneaking into Skinner's office, Remy finds some surprises among the piles of Gusteau memorabilia. Help Remy look for things the great chef left behind, as well as a few more recent items.

Gusteau's cookbook

News clipping about Linguini

Gusteau's first toque

Gusteau on a magazine cover

Letter from Linguini's mother

Gusteau's will

Linguini opens the door to the restaurant's walk-in refrigerator to find a surprise-rats! Emile has led the entire colony to Gusteau's, and now they are stealing all the food they can get their paws on. Look through the shelves of food to find these rats.

It is time for Linguini's big test! He must flabbergast the fussy taste buds of the famed food critic Ego. Look around the dining room of Gusteau's for these fine foods that are being served.

Prawns

Cheese plate

Pâté

Fancy vegetable dish

Leg of lamb

Chocolate mousse

Creep back into Skinner's office and look for these foods being sold under Gusteau's famous name.

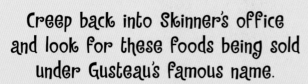

Haggis bites

Chicken nuggets

Corn dogs

BBQ meat

Burritos

Fried chicken

Step back into the walk-in refrigerator at Gusteau's to look for these fine foods.

Caviar

Cheese wheel

Grapes

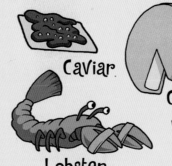
Lobster

Rib eye steaks

Fine chocolates

Sit back down in Gusteau's dining room and find...

Remy

Ego   Colette

Skinner in disguise

Linguini's roller skates

Pot of ratatouille